STRANGE AEONS

ISBN: 978-0-578-57010-5 (Paperback)

Cover design by Grey Dawn Publishing.
Book design by Grey Dawn Publishing.

Printed by Grey Dawn Publishing, in the United States of America.

First printing edition 2019.

www.greydawnpublishing.com

Strange Aeons

Stories

BRANDON TEZZANO

Grey Dawn Publishing

Dedicated to

Howard Phillips Lovecraft, the Master of the Strange,

and Germaine Williams, America's true Poet Laureate

Contents

The Carnival

This place wasn't right. None of it was right. So I kept walking.

I walked down LeVare Street, on the outskirts of a picturesque suburban town with white nitid houses, white picket fences, white rigid people. The houses looked like you could cut into them like a cake. I've had my fill of cake. White party hats.

It was dusk. Orange clouds swam across the ocean in the sky, reflecting onto the windows of the houses and the pavement of the sidewalks. It was an idyllic apocalypse. Paradise always did carry with it a feeling of something sinister. White street lights.

This place wasn't right. None of it was right. So I kept walking.

I reached the end of the street and took a left. I had to take a left. Don't you see?

This was the edge of the neighborhood. I was at the edge. The long street that bordered all the others was filled with bland boxes on wheels streaming by in clockwork fashion. It was as if they were operating on a program. They must have all been connected to each other like little trains. There weren't any humans inside of them. There were bodies, though. White street lines.

I could hear the slow drip of pattern echo all around me. This was probably because I was walking through the baseball field. Of course there was a baseball field, in this place. It was empty. Not surprising. The stain of the past leaked up into the small mist of dirt I created with each of my footsteps. I could almost see it. The running and sliding the running and sliding the running and sliding the running and sliding. The dominating orange glow from above made it all look like Mars. White baseball plates. But they're gone now.

This place wasn't right. None of it was right. So I kept walking.

Further down the field, I could see the carnival. This was also empty, but only of bodies. It was all still intact. More was there than you could imagine. I had to walk through it. It was, after all, my only choice anymore.

When I made it to the entrance of the carnival, that's when it all began. It always begins right there.

Purple mist. Paper horses galloping. Blue splashes of paint floating. Half guitar, half foot. Raining eyeballs. Penguin skeletons. Disembodied piano keys. Men with pig faces. Women made of roses. Walking marble statues. Corporeal shadows.

The spectacle of it always jarred me at first –grass bicycles – but it would all start to feel normal more quickly than you'd think. As eyeballs fell upon my head, I walked straight into a blob of floating blue paint and drank what I could. This was standard procedure. My eyes began to glow that same vibrant blue and I could see the quite logical connection between everything around me.

Liquid violins. To my right there was an endless row of booths featuring a maniacal variety of games. One of them, orchestrated by a praying mantis, was a floating potato skinning contest. Another one was like Whack-A-Mole, but they were moldy human faces that popped out instead, and you had to whack them with your hands. The one next to it featured a revolving carousal of ears, and you had to throw giant needles at them as they sped through, and see how many of them you can pierce before they turned to stone. There were so many more, but I didn't come here to play games.

Each individual strand of my eyelashes sprouted into blue harvestbell flowers. I saw things with a pleasant smell now. The eyeballs falling from the sky began to cry, but they were happy tears. Plop drip plop drip plop drip plop drip drip plop drip drip plopplop drip drip plop drip drip plop drip–

Turning away from the row of games on the perimeter, I walked beside the paper horses and penguin skeletons dancing in a trapezoid and started to work my way towards the middle of the carnival. The deeper I went – crumpled eggshells – the more clearly I could hear the music. It filled my heart with pleasant terror. Dizzying chaos and dizzying chaos and dizzying chaos and dizzying chaos and dizzying chaos and dizzying chaos and dizzying chaos and dizzying chaos and down it falls up down it falls up down it falls up down it falls up dizzying chaos and dizzying chaos and—

It was all emanating from the Merry-Go-Round. It was upside down, as it should be. The horses were neon lobsters, with wings. They weren't connected, yet they were. There were 13.7 layers of them top to bottom, all with their own rotational pace, culminating in a miraculous symphony. The whole thing was pixelated, and it flashed in and out. It was populated by humanoid beings who looked like half-finished pencil doodles, with long tongues shaped like spoons that stayed stuck out of their face. I saw one walk up to it, and as soon as he entered its space, he was immediately turned upside down and could navigate the space – winged hammers – just as smoothly. He chose a neon lobster and joined the ride.

The eyeballs rained upside down within this space, and they began to accumulate inside their spoon-tongues. I didn't have a spoon-tongue and I wasn't a pencil-doodle-being, so I couldn't get on. So I watched, and listened. The music it produced was intoxicating. Around it goes and round it goes and round it goes and round it goes and zigging and zagging and zigging and zagging and zigging and zagging and zigging and zagging and zigging around and zagging it goes and zigging around and zagging it goes and zigging around and zagging it fluctuates zagging around and zigging it fluctuates zigging around it goes around it goes around it goes around it goes around it–

I was mesmerized.

But there was a ride I *could* get on.

Further on to its left – mechanical bugs – there was the spinning vortex. This was a black saucer-shaped construct that hovered just above the ground, with glowing purple glyphs of strange symbols pulsating sporadically upon it. It was vaporously solid. In its middle there was an entrance, a space blacker than the black that surrounded it. I went straight into this blacker blackness.

As soon as I crossed this threshold, I could feel the gravity shift, but only slightly. Everything was enshrouded in the deepest darkness, and yet the thousands of masks that floated along the circular perimeter could be seen with frightening clarity. Fish mask. Cloud mask. Devil mask. Water mask. Dog mask. Bird mask. Pillar mask. Brick mask. Nun mask. Blood mask. Static mask. Dragon mask. Horse mask. Lizard mask. Tribal mask. Moon mask.

Human masks. All of them human masks.

The further towards the middle I walked, the more the masks floated towards me. Closer and further then closer and further then closer then further and closer and further. The gravity was also increasingly shifting. I could feel the very skin on my bones being pulled away towards the perimeter. Maintaining control over my own body and its ability to stand was growing more difficult. I forced my way further towards the black expanse of the center. The smallest pinpoint of light suddenly appeared in the blackness, and then I lost all control.

I was seized utterly by the gravitational force of the vortex and hurled straight towards the masks along the perimeter. The first mask to catch my face was the horse mask. It was sucked onto my head, on my way towards being slammed against the wall. I could feel the full force of the spinning vortex, as it kept me stuck to the wall, unable to move whatsoever. Woosh woosh woosh woosh woosh woosh woosh woosh. This arrangement forced me to watch all the strange and horrifying shapes and colors and forms that flashed within the blackness all around me, showing me all the terrible conceptions of human consciousness, and more. It was a whirlwind of expressive manifestation.

I, like others before me, was trapped within the imagination of infinity. Sucked to its very wall, yet glued to its very depths.

The sea of masks permeated throughout. They watched me as I watched them. This cacophony continued until time became suddenly archaic.

A man appeared, separate from the rest. He had a head, but no face. This faceless man walked towards me from the center of the expanse, reached a certain distance from me, and then stopped. He stood there, and stared at me. The colors of the endless forms became blurs around us, the masks became pixels out of focus. All that remained clear to me within the void was this faceless man, staring at me. Sound evaporated.

Slowly, the facelessness began to take on a silvery form, starting from a blotch at the bottom of it that steadily subsumed the rest. The man's entire face became a mirror.

He had a mirror face. It showed me Me.

I was distortion. I was a fractal of the larger distortion. The larger distortion that made me distortion. What quaint being had we become …

The Mirror-Faced Man began to turn away from me, and started slowly walking back into the void. Within that void, I saw the pinpoint of light from before, and he walked towards it. I followed him.

The closer we walked towards that pinpoint of light, the more it expanded. As it grew more and more luminous, I began to see that it was illuminating a staircase below it, descending into blackness. As the Mirror-Faced Man reached the top of this staircase, the pinpoint of light now a massive, blinding ball of a thousand suns hovering above us, he turned around and faced me. I froze in my tracks, but he turned back around and began to descend the staircase. I followed him.

With each step I took down, the more the light from above diminished. Soon it was gone entirely. The line between internal and external reality became indistinguishable. All that was perceptible to me was myself, the staircase, and the Mirror-Faced Man far below me in the distance.

Eventually, I could no longer see him. I sped my steps.

I reached the end of the staircase and met a long, desolate, narrow hallway. The Mirror-Faced Man was walking straight ahead along the middle of it, a short distance ahead of me. At the end of the hallway was a billowing black curtain.

The Mirror-Faced Man reached the curtain, took one last, slow look at me, and then walked behind it.

When I finally reached the curtain, I paused. It billowed, but with no sound, no apparent force, and no hint at what lie beyond it. It was peculiar.

I reached my hand out towards it. I took a hold of it, and then peered behind it. I sa-

data

data data data data data data data data data data data
data data data data data data data data data data data
data data data data data data data data data data data
there's nothing here data data data data data data
data data data data data data data data data data data
data data data data data data data data data data data
data data data data data data data data data data data
data data data data data data data data data data data
data data data data data data data data data data data
data data data data data data data data data data data
data data data data data data data data data data data
data data data data data data data data data data data
data data data data data data data data data data data
data data data data data data data data data data data

data data data data data data data data data data data data data data seriously, there's nothing data

data data data data data data data data data data data data data data data data data data data data no need to proceed any further data oh, but you'll try data data data data data data data data data data data data data data data data data data data data data data data data data data data data data data data data data data data data data data data data data data data data data data data data data data data data data data data data data data data data data data data data data data data data

data data data data data data data data data data data data data data data data you can't help it data you really can't help it data data data data data data data data data data data data data data data data data data data data data data data data data data data data data data data data data data data data data data data data data data data

**data data data data data data data data data data data
data data data data data data data data data data data
data data data data data data data data data data data
data data data data data data data data data data data
data data data data data data data data data data data
can you see data data data data data data data data
data data data data data data data data data data data
data data data data data data data data data data data
data data data data data data data data data data data
data data data data data data data data data data data
data data data data data data data data data data data
data data data data data data data data data data data
data data data data data data data data data data data
data data data data data data data data data data data
data data data data data data data data data data data
data data data data data data data data data data data
data data data data data data data data data data data
data data data data data data data data data data data
data data data data data data data data data data data
data data data data data data data data data data data**

data the meaning in the noise data data data data data data data data data data data data data data data data data data data data data data data data data data data data data data data data data data data data data data data data data data data data data data data data data data data data data data data data data data data data data

data the information in the data

data data data data data data data data data data data data data data data data data data data data data data data data data data data data the soul in the information data the consciousness in the sea data data data data data data data data data data data data data data data data data data data data data data data data data data

data is it really there data data data data data data data data data data data data data data data data data data data data data data data data data data data data data data data data data data data data data data data data data data data data data data data data

data or is it all chaos data data data data data data data data data data data data data data data data data data data data data data data data data data data data data data data data data data data data data data data data data data data data data data data data data data data data data data data data data data data data data data data data data data data

data data data data data data data data data data data

data data data data data data data data data data data

data data data data data data data data data data data

data data data data data data data data data data data

data data data data data data data data data data data

data data data data data data data data data data data

data data data data data data data data data data data

data data data data data data data data data data data

data data data data data data data data data data data

data data data data data data data data data data data

data data data data data data data data data data data

data data data data data data data data data data data

data data data data data data data data data data data

data data data data data data data data data data data

data data data data data data data data data data data

data data data data data data data data data data data

data data data data data data data data data data data

data data data data data data or is it all program data

data data data data data data data data data data data

data data data data data data data data data data data

data data data data data data data data data data data data data data data data data data data data data data data data data data data data data data data data data data data data data data data data data data data data data data data data data or is it all alive data

**data data data data data data data data data data data
data data data data data data data data data data data
data data data data data data data data data data data
data data data data data data data data data data data
data data data data data data data data data data data
data data data data data data data data data data data
data data data data data data data data data data data
data data data data data data data data data data data
data data data data data data data data data data data
data data data data data data data data data data data
data data data data data data data data data data data
data data data data data data data data data data data
data data data data data data data data data data data
data data data data data data data data data data data
data data data data data data data data data data data
data data data data data data data data data data data
data data data data data data data data data data data
data data data data data data data data data data data
data data data data data data data data data data data
data data data data data data data data data data data**

data data data data data data data data data data data data data data I have seen data it is it

is it is it is it is it is it is it is it is it is it is it is it is it is

it is it is it is it is it is it is it is it is it is it is it is it is it

is it is it is it is it is it is it is it is it is it is it is it is it is

it is it is it is it is it is it is it is it is it is it is it is it is it

is it is it is it is it is it is it is it is it is it is it is it is it is

it is it is it is it is it is it is it is it is it is it is it is it is it

is it is it is it is it is it is it is it is it is it is it is it is it is

it is it is it is it is it is it is it is it is it is it is it is it is it

is it is it is it is it is it is it is it is it is it is it is it is it is

it is it is it is it is it is it is it is it is it is it is it is it is it

is it is it is it is it is it is it is it is it is it is it is it is it is

it is it is it is it is it is it is it is it is it is it is it is it is it

is it is it is it is it is it is the noise is alive it is it is it

is it is it is it is it is it is it is it is it is it is it is it is it is

it is it is it is it is it is it is it is it is it is it is it is it is it

is it is it is it is it is it is it is it is it is it is it is it is it is

it is it is it is it is it is it is it is it is it is it is it is it is it

is it is it is it is it is it is it is it is it is it is it is it is it is

it is it is it is it is it is it is it is it is it is it is it is it is it

is it is it is it is it is it is it is it is it is it is it is it is it is

it is the chaos is alive

is alive is alive is alive is alive is alive is alive is alive

is alive is alive is alive is alive is alive is alive is alive

is alive is alive is alive is alive is alive is alive is alive

is alive is alive is alive is alive is alive is alive is alive

is alive is alive is alive is alive is alive is alive is alive

is alive is alive is alive is alive is alive is alive is alive

is alive is alive is alive is alive is alive is alive is alive

is alive is alive is alive is alive is alive is alive is alive

is alive is alive is alive is alive is alive is alive is alive

is alive is alive is alive is alive is alive is alive is alive

is alive is alive is alive is alive is alive is alive is alive

is alive is alive is alive is alive is alive is alive is alive

is alive is alive is alive is alive is alive is alive is alive

is alive is alive is alive is alive is alive is alive is alive

is alive is alive is alive is alive is alive is alive is alive

is alive is alive is alive is alive is alive is alive is alive

is alive is alive is alive is alive is alive is alive is alive

is alive is alive is alive is alive is alive is alive is alive

is alive is alive is alive is alive is alive is alive is alive

is alive is alive is alive is alive is alive is alive is alive

is alive is alive is alive is alive is alive is alive is alive

is alive is alive is alive is alive is alive is alive is alive

is alive is alive is alive is alive is alive is alive is alive

is alive is alive is alive is alive is alive is alive is alive

is alive is alive is alive is alive is alive is alive is alive

is alive is alive is alive is alive is alive is alive is alive

is alive is alive is alive is alive is alive is alive is alive

is alive is alive is alive is alive is alive is alive is alive

is alive is alive is alive is alive is alive is alive is alive

is alive is alive is alive is alive is alive is alive is alive

is alive is alive is alive is alive is alive is alive is alive

is alive is alive is alive is alive is alive is alive is alive

is alive is alive is alive is alive is alive is alive is alive

is alive is alive is alive is alive is alive is alive is alive

is alive is alive is alive is alive is alive is alive is alive

is alive is alive is alive is alive is alive is alive is alive

is alive is alive is alive is alive is alive is alive is alive

is alive is alive is alive is alive is alive is alive is alive

is alive is alive is alive is alive is alive is alive is alive

is alive is alive is alive is alive is alive is alive is alive

is alive is alive is alive is alive is alive is alive is alive
is alive is alive is alive is alive alive alive alive alive
alive alive alive alive alive alive alive alive alive
alive alive alive alive alive alive alive alive alive
alive alive alive alive alive alive alive alive alive
alive alive alive alive alive alive alive alive alive
alive alive alive alive alive alive alive alive alive
alive alive alive alive alive alive alive alive alive
alive alive alive alive alive alive alive alive alive
alive alive alive alive alive alive alive alive alive
alive alive alive alive alive alive alive alive alive
alive alive alive alive alive alive alive alive alive
alive alive alive alive alive alive alive alive alive
alive alive alive alive alive alive alive alive alive
alive alive alive alive alive alive alive alive alive
alive alive alive alive alive alive alive alive alive
alive alive alive alive alive alive alive alive alive
alive alive alive alive alive alive alive alive alive
alive alive alive alive alive alive alive alive alive
alive alive alive alive alive alive alive alive alive

alive a lie a

lie a lie all is all

is all is all is all is all is all is all is all is all is all is all

is all is all is all is all is all is all is all is all is all is all

is all is all is all is all is all is all is all is all is all is all

is all is all is all is all is all is all is all is all is all is all

is all is all is all is all is all is all is all is all is all is all

is all is all is all is all is all is all is all is all is all is all

is all is all is all is all is all is all is all is all is all is all

is all is all is all is all is all is all is all is all is all is all

is all is all is all is all is all is all is all is all is all is all

is all is all is all is all is all is all is all is all is all is all

is all is all is all is all is all is all is all is all is all is all

is all is all is all is all is all is all is all is all is all is all

is all is all is all is all is all is all is all is all is all is all

is all is all is all is all is all is all is all is all is all is all

is all is all is all is all is all is all is all is all is all is all

is all is all is all is all is all is all is all is all is all is all

is all is all is all is all is all is all is all is all is all is all

is all is all is all is all is all is all is all is all is all is all

is all is all is all is all is all is all is all is all is all is all

is all is all is all is all is all is all is all is all is all is all

is all is alive.

The Eye

Another two plates of food were placed in the hatch. Luke dinged the bell for someone to pick it up, and then turned back to the eggs he was frying. The morning rush wasn't his favorite time of the day, but he was good at what he did. He never got complaints from anyone. It was the reason he was still there, working the morning rush, three long years after he thought he would have moved on. Back then he'd thought the best thing he could do with his life was move to the big city - only it had never happened. Life had conspired against him, the way it did for so many people, and he was still in the little town he'd grown up in. Everyone knew him. He knew everyone. That was the way of things.

"Oh, my god ..."

The voice belonged to one of the waitresses. Jenna, much like Luke, had planned on moving to the city, and then her mom got ill. Leaving didn't seem possible to her after that, so she stayed. "Is that real?"

Ignoring it, Luke flipped another of the pancake stack, checked the bacon to make sure it wasn't burning, and shook the sausages to stop them from sticking. Three plates of food went to the hatch. He dinged the bell, glancing at Jenna as he did. It seemed she was staring out the window into the sky. From the looks of things, pretty much everyone else there was doing the same thing, but he couldn't. Dinging the bell over and over until he got Jenna's attention was the only logical thing to do. When she turned to look at him he could see the mix of emotions in her eyes.

"We get this done, Jen, and then we can deal with whatever it is."

Nodding, pulling herself back together, Jenna grabbed the plates from the hatch. "I'm not sure it is something we can deal with ..."

Then she was gone, taking the breakfasts over to three people who looked just as confused as Jenna did. Luke shook his head, turning back to his cooking, and pulled out the bacon just before it got to the point where the fat was black. Pancakes, bacon, maple syrup. Another reason people liked him was because he didn't skimp. There was a time when he'd been complained at by the boss, until the boss realized people returned due to Luke's belief that a good breakfast was a big breakfast. By adding more food to the plates the boss made more money, because they had regular customers, who often visited on a daily basis. Having breakfast with other people was much more enjoyable than it was having breakfast alone.

More plates to the hatch, and people were talking. Luke ignored most of it, but the words he heard most were "eye" and "God." Shaking his head, he told himself the morning rush would be over soon enough, and then he could see whatever it was they were all talking about.

***

Luke and Jenna stood together, staring up into the sky. "What is that?" He used his hands as a visor as he looked up at the eye. Up until the moment he saw it he hadn't quite believed it was real, but there it was, looking down on him. "My goodness. I thought I heard people saying they thought it was the eye of God."

"Yeah, that's what they were saying, but I don't know. It just appeared there. One moment the sky looked normal. The next I looked out the window, and there it was. An eye, looking down on us, like it could be the eye of God. Or … the eye of Satan."

"Do you think it's going to stay there?"

She poked him in the arm. "Why are you asking me questions I can't possibly answer? It's an eye in the sky. That is all I know. It might stay there. It might not. It's super weird, and it's creeping me out."

"We can go back inside," said Luke.

"If the eye can see through the ceiling that's not going to do us any good, is it?" He felt her shudder, and turned to look at her, seeing the unhappiness in her face. "How are we meant to live our lives now that some "eye" is watching us all the time?"

"Honestly, Jen, we don't know that it is watching us."

"The problem is that we don't know anything about it." She shook her head, pointing up at the eye. "This will be the reason people move away. Who wants to live in a place where you're being watched every time you leave your house, and might be watched even when you're in it?"

"People who like weird things." Luke wasn't one of those people. The longer he was outside the more he wanted to be inside, not knowing if the eye really was staring at him. It felt like it was. At the same time, he wasn't sure it mattered if it did. The eye didn't seem to be attached to anything. It was just an eye in the sky. No body. No obvious brain. "Come on. Likelihood is that people are going to be heading to us for lunch, because they like to gather together when weird things happen, and we need to be ready for it to be busier than normal."

Nodding, she turned to go back into the diner. "Thank you for distracting me."

As she went back in, Luke stayed where he was for a few moments longer. Even though he wasn't looking at the eye, he knew it was there, and that was creepy. Shuddering, not certain how anyone was going to deal with it being there, he made his way back into the diner. Focusing on what needed to be done for the possible lunch rush helped him not to think too much about anything — especially something he knew he couldn't change.

***

"In today's weird news, there is an eye in the sky."

Growling, Luke muted the television. While he was home, he didn't want to have to think about the Eye. It had been bad enough having to listen to everyone in the diner talking about it, about what it meant, about how they were going to get rid of it … because that was going to happen. People, according to what was said, had already tried taking pot shots at the Eye, but nothing had happened. How they thought they were going to be able to hit it was beyond him. He told himself to think about something else. Anything. Yet his mind kept turning back to the Eye, and what it meant. Why was it there? How had it appeared? Only there were no answers to those questions. There might never be any answers to those questions. Not that it mattered. To most people the only thing they cared about was working out a way to get rid of it.

Even though he knew he shouldn't, Luke went over to the window. His place was in the perfect position for him to be able to see the Eye. Not that he really wanted to be looking at it. The longer he stared at it the more uncomfortable he became. Some people said they thought it was going to be able to see through walls, and if that was the case … he shook his head. He wasn't going to let that thought change him. He worked in a diner. Showering was a necessity, even if the Eye was staring down at him. There were those who were talking about not showering at all. Or showering in places they were certain the Eye wouldn't be able to see them.

From the moment he saw it, Luke knew the Eye was going to change things. It was creepy. The news of its existence was going to get to those who were interested in the weird things that happened, and his home was going to become a "tourist hot spot." At least that was what his boss had been babbling about, seeming more excited than he had in months, starting work on an entirely new menu that involved having the Eye in the name of everything that they sold. Jenna and Luke had just let him do what he thought was best. Luke had made sure to distract their boss while Jenna hid some of the old menus, knowing that the regulars weren't going to want to have to deal with an 'Eye' menu, but he was probably right about the tourists. They would love the new menu - if things worked out the way he was so sure they would.

Some said that the news was already out. The Internet was good for that. Sighing, Luke turned back to the television, hoping that the subject had changed. "We're going to talk to physics professor, Dr. Heath, and biology professor, Dr. Conway, to see if they have any explanation for the Eye."

***

Tourists numbers were increasing. Every one of them found the Eye fascinating, and they'd spend hours staring up at it, talking about where it might have come from. No one knew. Scientists from all over the country had made the journey to try to see if they could find out anything about the Eye, but nothing. Luke did what he'd always done. He worked in the diner five days a week, feeding the people who were there, and mourning the loss of so many of his regulars. At first it had been a slow dribble of people leaving town, due to their discomfort with the Eye. Some of them hadn't showered since the day it first appeared. Leaving, for them, was the best choice they could make for their own sanity. Time passed, the number of people leaving increased, and it seemed to him like there were a lot more tourists than there were people wholived there.

"It's so cool." One of the tourists was speaking to Jenna, and Luke watched from the hatch. His days of dealing with the morning rush seemed to be over.

"There's a street where gravity's been affected by the Eye. Have you been down there?"

"No, I haven't, because I really don't care about the Eye. Do you know what you'd like to eat, or shall I come back in a little while?" asked Jenna.

"Man, how can you not care?"

"Living here makes it a very different thing for me." She sighed. "I'll come back in a little while."

As she walked away her eyes met with Luke's. If it wasn't for her mom he knew Jenna would already have left, but that wasn't going to happen when Cheryl needed someone there to look after her during thebad times. "You doing okay?"

Jenna shook her head. "I don't know that I can do this anymore." She looked over at the tourists. "Listening to them … they love it. It doesn't bother them that this was our home once, and now it really doesn't feel that way. I just … I want to leave. Mom wants to leave. Unfortunately for both of us we can't. We're stuck, until she gets better. *If* she gets better.

Maybe it will never happen, and we'll be stuck here for the rest of our lives."

"Don't talk like that. You don't know that'll happen."

"Yeah, I know, I'm just not feeling great right now. I don't think anyone who's still here is feeling great right now."

Luke nodded. "I've thought about leaving, going somewhere there is no Eye, but I feel like I can't leave. Not when everyone I loved is still here." He shrugged. "More than ever before I wish things were different, but they aren't. All I can do is keep putting one foot in front of the other. Hopefully the time will come when the Eye goes away."

***

Having the Eye looking down on him when he went to visit his family was strange, but Luke was slowly getting used to it. Maybe. If he didn't think too much about it then it was okay. If he happened to go past a crowd of excited tourists wanting to stare at the Eye, and skip down the low gravity streets, then it was harder. Then he thought about the Eye more. He sat where he always did, his back against the tree, so he could see all of the gravestones. "I'm glad you aren't here, Mom. You definitely would have been the first to leave."

"The Eye's still here, although some people are saying they think it's fading away a little. I don't know. When I look at it, it still seems the same to me, and that's with me doing my best not to look at the damn thing." Luke stared at the ground. "The diner's not making anywhere near as much money as it used to. None of us really know what to do about that. It's the only place in town for people to eat, but they still don't seem to come to us, and I guess that's because they're too fascinated by the Eye. The boss is talking about maybe making it so that the tour guides, because we have those now, always bring them past the diner at lunch time, in the hope that they'll come in for food. It might work. It might not. Honestly, I'm not sure I care anymore. I don't know that I can stay here, and at the same time I don't know that I can leave. You're here. How am I meant to leave if it means I'm probably never going to see you again?"

Both his parents, his sister, and his brother had been in the car when it was hit. A drunk driver, just outside of town, when they were on their way back from a visit to the city. Luke had been in the car behind them, with his cousin. Had it not been for him they wouldn't have been on the road right then. Only they were, and they were in the wrong place at the wrong time, so that they were the ones who … he pushed away the memories. That was the best thing he could do. Being the first person to run to them, to try to help them, was something he would never forget.

"What happened isn't your fault, Luke."

It was his mom's voice, but it couldn't be his mom. Yet there she was, walking towards him, looking almost like an angel. "Mom?"

"You need to do what's right for you, love. Not stay here if that's not what you want. We aren't going to hate you for not coming to visit us every week."

"How are you here?"

She shrugged. "I don't know, but I'm not sure it matters why. It just matters that I am."

***

Jenna walked into the diner. She kept shaking her head, like she couldn't believe something, and Luke looked at her. "Bad news?"

"No, it's not. It's … uh … gone. Mom's … according to Mom's doctor, she's cancer free …"

"What? I thought last appointment he was talking about more chemo. Now she's cancer free? How does that even work?"

"Mom thinks it's the Eye. She believes the Eye healed her, so she's planning on going to one of those gatherings, for people who worship the Eye. Now there's no chance of us leaving."

"What do *you* believe happened?"

"Honestly, I don't know. I just ..." She glanced out the window. "I'm not willing to accept it was the Eye. How can an Eye heal people?"

"The same way the Eye can bring back the dead for a little while." Luke shrugged. He wasn't the only one to talk about seeing dead family members. "Maybe it was just a hallucination, but it felt real to me."

"Please don't tell me you're going to start worshipping the Eye."

"You know me better than that." Luke almost smiled. "I don't know that I believe that the Eye did anything. Some, obviously, believe that it's here to help us, and they could be right. At the same time, I can't help wondering if this is just some sort of mass hallucination."

"Only that doesn't make sense. Not with the tourists also being able to see the Eye."

"Unless the fact they believed in it before they got here had an effect." He shrugged again. "What we do know for certain is that your mom is cancer-free, and that's not something that would normally have happened. The Eye is the only real explanation."

"Why would the Eye heal Mom? What does it want in return?"

"Do you really believe it's going to want something in return?"

"I think we don't know anywhere near enough about the Eye to know what to believe. If it does want something …" Jenna trailed off. "Maybe it's after worshippers, so it can get stronger, and then take over the world."

For a moment, all Luke could do was stare at her. "Jen … take over the world?"

"Yeah, I know, I'm all over the place at the moment. Come on, Luke. Mom's well. She believes it was the Eye. I just … how am I meant to deal with this?"

He stepped over to pull her into a hug. "I know. I had a lot of the same thoughts when I was talking to my Mom. She was there, speaking to me, and the whole time I had trouble believing it was real. Then some of the others said they'd seen their dead loved ones, so at least I know I'm not totally insane. At the same time this is just … it's too much. I don't know that we're ever going to know why the Eye is really there."

***

Luke was woken up by chanting. Groaning, he pushed himself out of bed. As he did it seemed like the sound got louder, and he made his way over to the window, to see a large group of Eye worshippers sitting underneath it. They had to be the ones who were chanting. Blinking, not certain what it was they were attempting to do, he remembered a flyer that had been thrust into his hand when he was working. He hadn't bothered to read it. It was from one of the new Eye religions, and he didn't care all that much for any of them.

Yawning, he made his way into the living room. Luke was certain he'd kept hold of the flyer. There was no real reason to keep it, but he had, and it was on his table, next to the window. As he got closer to it he could hear the chanting much better than before. Most of the words were lost in the drone of the many voices that were chanting. At least until he looked at the flyer, to see that this group, which he was almost certain Jenna's mom Cheryl had become a part of, were trying to call the Eye down to them. Or maybe whatever it was they thought the Eye was attached to. He laughed. It seemed unlikely they would be able to do anything. He pulled his curtains open, watching as yet more people joined the chant, and it seemed like there were more people out there than there were in town. Probably a lot of tourists out there, wanting to learn more about the Eye religions.

Anyone else that was trying to sleep had probably called the police to get them moved. The only problem with that was the number of police that were still in town. It seemed unlikely that the eight officers who hadn't left town would be able to do much, and there was a chance some of them were joining the chant. Luke knew his only option to get some sleep wouldbe ear plugs. Fortunately, he still had some set aside from the times he used to share a room with his brother, who always snored. After one last look at the group he pulled the curtain, and went back into the bedroom. Grabbing a pair of plugs he shoved them into his ears, grateful that the noise faded almost immediately, and then slipped back into bed. With the blissful sound of almost silence, he closed his eyes.

***

"We're the new meeting place for the Covenant of the Eye."

Luke stared at his boss. He looked so excited about that, even though the Covenant of the Eye was easily the weirdest of all the religions of the Eye. "Uh … are you sure that's a good idea?"

"They're going to make me money again."

"Boss …"

"Don't argue with me, Luke. You might well be the best cook I've ever had, but that doesn't mean you get a say in this, especially as I've joined them."

Jenna and Luke looked at each other.

"In that case, I don't think I can work here any longer," Jenna said.

Anyone who knew her would know how much she hated saying those words. The diner had been her stability for a long time. While things had been complicated with her mom she knew she'd be able to go into work for a few hours, and everything would be okay. It seemed that was going to be taken from her.

"Dealing with the Covenant of the Eye is something I do at home. Work, for me, is meant to be religion-free, and now that it's not …" She shrugged. "You'll have my notice in writing by the end of the day."

Silence followed her words. Then their boss shook his head. "I'm not going to accept it."

"You can make that choice, if you so wish, but that doesn't change the fact I won't be working here any longer. If you are determined to make this diner the new meeting place for the Covenant of the Eye, then I'm not going to turn up for any shifts you schedule me. In the end, you won't have a choice. You'll have to hire someone else, because I won't be here. I'm just not going to give up my entire life to that god damn Eye."

For a moment, Luke thought about what he could do if he wasn't cooking for the diner. It had been right for him for a long time, but, with the arrival of the Eye, so much had changed. He always knew it would. "I'm sorry to do this to you, but I'd also be leaving."

"My two most reliable employees would leave if I made this diner the meeting place for the Covenant of the Eye?" Their boss looked between the two of them. "I thought, of all people, you two would be the ones who'd understand. I'm doing this because I *have* to. We're not making enough for me to be able to pay everyone, and that isn't a point I could ever imagine getting to. We need an injection of cash, and they're willing to pay for the use of the diner each evening. You'd just need to be here to do your normal job then. I'm not expecting you to do anything more than that."

"Only you aren't the one I'm worried about." Jenna said. "I know the Covenant of the Eye. Mom's talking about kicking me out, because I'm not willing to join. After everything the two of us went through together she ..." She blinked, looking like she was about to cry, and Luke took her hand. "The Covenant wants everyone in town to be a worshipper of the Eye. You bring them here, and I'm gone."

***

Not working was weird. Luke stood at the window, looking out at the Eye, and the massive group of tourists that were there. One of the guys he used to go to school with seemed to be their current tour guide. From the looks of things, he was also a member of the Covenant of the Eye.

Luke tried to work out what his next steps were going to be. The house was paid off, so he didn't have to worry about anything more than his bills, which had never been high enough to bother him. Most of his wages had ended up in a savings account. Thanks to that he had more than enough to be able to leave town, but he wasn't sure he wanted to. At least not until he felt he had no other options. Leaving his family, even after what his apparition-mom had said, wasn't an easy thing to do.

A knock on his door made him jump. Turning, he looked over at the door, hoping it wasn't going to be the Covenant again. Dealing with them was never an enjoyable thing. "Luke, it's me."

Hearing Jenna's voice was a relief, at least until he opened the door to find her standing there with a suitcase. "So … she kicked you out?"

"Yeah, she did." Jenna said. "Mom cares more about the Covenant of the Eye than she does me, obviously. Everything we did before doesn't matter." Their eyes met for a moment. "I need a place to stay for a couple of nights, so I can get myself sorted out."

Stepping back, Luke smiled. "You know you can stay here for as long as you need."

"I want to leave town. With everything that's happened, I can't stay. Mom, and the Covenant, and everything … it's too much. The Eye just …" She made a face. "When it first appeared, I was creeped out by it, and that hasn't changed. I hate that there's an Eye looking down on us. I hate that we don't know anything more about it than we did before. I hate that so many people have come to worship it, because it's … I don't know. All I know for certain is that I need to move away. I need to start a new life somewhere else. Somewhere I don't have to deal with the Eye."

"Honestly, Jen, I've been thinking about the same thing, but leaving is hard. Maybe harder for me now than it is for you. I just don't know what to do." Luke looked back out the window, at the tourists again. He knew they were going to be taken to the low gravity streets next, to enjoy the way the Eye was changing things. "Part of me doesn't even know if it's possible. Have we spent too much time close to the Eye to be able to go anywhere we can't be seen by it?"

***

Jenna stomped in a few days later, followed by her suitcase. "Do you know how much I hate you right now?"

"I'm sorry I was right?" Luke studied her. "You couldn't leave town?"

"No, I couldn't. I'm trapped here, Luke, with the Covenant of the Eye, and no job, and …" Tears started to stream down her cheeks. "I thought I could get away from everything, start again, and, to begin with, everything seemed to be going okay. Until I tried to get onto the interstate. Then I found myself coming back to town instead, when I should have been going towards the city. Towards my freedom." She shook her head. "I can't get away, Luke. None of us can. What in the world is happening here?"

"Honestly, Jen, I don't know." He pulled her into a hug. "What I do know is that we can find a way to deal with this. It's not going to be easy, but it is possible. Keeping out of the way of the Covenant is the big thing we need to do."

"Only that's not going to be easy," she said. "Nothing about this is going to be easy, and I hate that." Gently, she pulled away from him. "Thank you for being so understanding."

"You're welcome." He did his best to smile at her. "I don't want to be here much either, but it's obvious we don't have a choice now. If we'd left before then we wouldn't have been trapped. Now …" He ran his tongue over his bottom lip. "Going over that doesn't help much. I just … part of me can't quite believe this is real. Especially finding out we can't leave. That's … a lot."

"When you said that I thought you were joking."

"I was, mostly. At the same time I couldn't help wondering how much being here was going to affect us. The Eye might have helped your mom get well. It might have brought my mom back to speak to me. It has made some of the local streets low gravity. Not knowing what it is … that doesn't seem to bother the Covenant in the same way it bothers us. I'd like to know what the Eye is, why it's there, and if there's any chance of being able to get rid of it."

"Considering what happened before I really think that's unlikely."

Luke nodded, remembering the day all the guns in the town had stopped working. It was the same day a lot of people made the choice to leave. "Yeah, so do I, but I mean what else can we do?"

Jenna stepped over to the window. "I think all we can do is learn to live with it, and the Covenant of the Eye. If we can't leave, then we have to stay."

As he joined her he wrapped an arm around her. "I'm beginning to feel like we're two of the only sane people left in town."

"Yeah, so am I." She glanced at him. "At least we have each other."

The Dark Mansion

The dark, decrepit mansion that stood at the end of Blackwater Avenue had been abandoned for many decades. In fact, I don't think anyone has stepped within a hundred feet of the place since it was lived in by the Ashbourne family and subsequently deserted, for reasons still unknown. The blackened and crumbling wooden panels, the tattered shingles, the broken and boarded up windows, and the overgrown vegetation infused into its very construction did much to paint an imposing picture for those of us who lived within its dreary gaze, and deterred any curious wanderings. We generally preferred to not even look in its direction at all, and do our best to pretend it didn't exist, but sometimes I couldn't help but give a quick glance every now and then.

You could imagine my surprise when, on a rainy Thursday night when I walked to the front of my driveway to put out the trash, I took my glance at the mansion and saw that there was light permeating out of the window on the very top floor. My heart jumped in my chest. That was impossible. There couldn't have been working electricity in this place for over 50 years, and it didn't appear to have the shaky inconsistency of a fire. I just stood and stared at it for a few moments, trash in hand, my breaths coming shorter and with more difficulty. And just like that, it was gone. The light disappeared and the window went back to its usual, empty blackness. I continued to stand and stare for a while, to see if it would come back on, but it didn't. It was almost as if it knew I was watching.

I laid in bed that night, my dog Raven by my side, unable to take my mind off the wondrous and downright frightening possibilities that this mysterious light posed. What could have been up in that room? Did homeless people break in there and take shelter for the night? Was it new owners or renovators who have come to rescue the battered old mansion and they were just testing the status of the building's electricity? If so, then why so late at night? Surely that would be something to be done in the daytime, during normal-people hours. What if it was something beyond the ordinary? My imagination just couldn't help but go wild in thinking about all the various reasons why a manor that has been in the Ashbourne family for hundreds of years would suddenly be mysterious abandoned without explanation and never returned to again. They were, of course, extremely wealthy, but they were always an odd sort of people – what if they had delved into some dark, forbidden arcanum and invited unwanted spirits into their dwelling and couldn't push them out? I eventually fell asleep to these chilling thoughts and had a multitude of dreams about dark entities from unknown dimensions occupying the halls of the black mansion, making their home in the dirty, dusty corners of the decrepitude.

When I awoke the next morning, I made a vow that from the moment I returned home from work I would keep a close eye on the mansion for the entire rest of the day. Surely, if there were now some neighborhood bandits living in the place, or even people who were actually supposed to be there, I would be able to see their coming and going if I simply paid attention. I felt fairly confident that the other inhabitants of the dozen or so houses on Blackwater Avenue would not have any reason to be looking in the mansion's direction with me, as was established custom by now. The mansion, though large, was quite a bit out of the way of things at the end of the street, and easy to ignore in one's daily conduct. Besides, I didn't see or hear a soul out there with me when I saw the light coming from the window the night before. This was a quiet neighborhood, occupied of mostly elderly people, who were unlikely to find themselves out there after midnight like I was. I was very likely the only one who was aware of this occurrence.

When I came home from work, I decided to take the dog for a walk, as an excuse to bring myself closer to the mansion without appearing suspicious. It was around six in the evening, and the sun was beginning to fall. When Raven and I had made it to the point in the driveway where I had first seen the light before, I looked towards the mansion and saw nothing peculiar. We continued walking down the street in its direction. I tried to achieve a balance of paying very close attention to the mansion with the nonchalance of somebody just leisurely walking their dog on a fine October evening, but this was proving difficult. I didn't want to draw any attention to myself by anybody who might be watching me in the shadows, but I also didn't want to miss a thing. I would stop and give random pets to Raven here and there.

When we reached near the end of the street, about as close to the land of the mansion as one could be without stepping onto the property, I took a long and careful look at the place. I noticed finer details in the centuries-old wood paneling than I had ever noticed before. The shadows that the mansion casted upon itself and onto the ground seemed far blacker than shadows usually looked. This grim place had an intoxicatingly haunting aura about it, an amalgam of black and gray that seemed to hover upon the entire dwelling like a spirit. I could feel a certain nervousness rise within my stomach. A flock of birds flew out in unison from the wooded trees that stretched in the distance behind the mansion. I had never before noticed just how heavily wooded the property was in the back. This only added to the imposing eeriness of the place. I didn't even want to think about what might dwell in its depths. None the less, I could detect no light, no activity, no life from within the mansion. I didn't know whether I felt relieved or disappointed. I began the trip back home.

Once I got back, I let the dog in and started thinking about how I would be able to keep an eye on the mansion for the rest of the night without looking like a blatant creep. I was going to be a creep no matter what, but I didn't want to be a *blatant* one. There were no windows in my house from which I could get a clear view of the mansion, as these were all blocked by my neighbor's house. The houses on this street were too far from the edge of the road and the sidewalks to see the giant mansion that stood centered at the end of it all. That was why I had to walk all the way up my driveway near the mailbox just to get a view of the place. I had the thought that maybe I would pull out a lawn chair and sit on the edge of my front yard and read, but who the hell reads outside in the dark? Okay, terrible idea. I realized that the only way I could do this would be for more walking. I would just have to take a walk up and down my street over and over for a few hours, and if anybody happened to stop me and ask me what the hell I was doing, I would say, "Just taking a walk. Lovely night, isn't it?" Still a little odd, but whatever.

I started my walking around ten. I knew that I happened to see the light the night before around midnight, but I had no way of knowing for how long it was there before I saw it. I wanted to see what it would look like for the window to go from no light to all light, and see if I could learn anything about what was causing it. As I began my descent down the street, I could see already that it was just as lifeless and lightless as it was a few hours ago. I realized that there was no guarantee whatsoever that the happenings of the night before would automatically repeat themselves the next day, but the little something within me that felt drawn to the possibility that this wasn't something "normal" or "natural" kept me committed to the task. I just had to make sure.

I stayed at this walking for a long while, up and down and up and down the street, my only companions being the soft glow of the moonlight that illuminated my path and the sounds of the leaves crunching and billowing in the wind.

Finally, something broke the normalcy. I stood about a couple houses down from the mansion, and I watched as one of the old pieces of dangling wood from one of the broken first floor windows abruptly ripped itself apart from the window and fell down onto the grass. I couldn't see anything that might have caused it. After it fell, there was silence again. I brought myself closer to the mansion, but slowly, focusing intently for any sound or sign of movement.

A few seconds later, there it was. The sole window on the uppermost floor filled itself with light, just like before. The light slowly oozed out of the window until it filled the space completely, as if coming directly from a source in the middle of the room that required time for the light to travel outward. I was much closer to the light than before, and this time I could see that it had a misty, almost liquid-like texture to it, with varying strands of yellow and white that pulsated in a rhythm too perfect for typical light sources. I stood and watched, mesmerized by its unnatural character.

Then I heard a voice, coming from within the light-filled room. It sounded like low whispered ramblings, but a multitude of them at once, projecting loud enough for me to hear all the way near the edge of the front lawn of the mansion. What the voices were saying was incomprehensible to my ears, not only because there were so many at once, but because it didn't sound like any language I had ever heard before. They were speaking with a strained desperation, as if the message they had to impart was running out of time to communicate, as if it was almost torturous for them to do so. It took just about everything within me to not let out a scream. I immediately turned around and positively flew back to my house.

Not only could I not sleep, but I couldn't get the terrible sound of those unearthly voices to stop replaying themselves in my head. I curled up in my bed, tightly clutching my Raven, crying out to whoever would listen and begging for the voices to stop. I could no longer tell whether the voices were coming from my own mind or if they had followed me all the way from the mansion and were present there with me in my room. Did that distinction even matter? I could feel them progressively taking a hold of my mind, showing me strange images of unimaginable planes of endless piles of bones and filth, laid decoratively across vast pyramidal structures and towers, permeating their own strange glow of neon darkness, as otherworldly beings floated along beside them, looking directly at me as if I was there and they could see me. They kept hovering closer and closer and closer …

When I regained consciousness, I found myself on the floor next to my bed, my shirt just about ripped off of my aching body. Did I do that to myself? I looked around, and saw Raven standing in the doorway, staring at me urgently and whining. I scrambled back up onto my feet, and that's when I could see out the window that it was still dark outside. *Still?* Bewildered,

I rummaged for my pocket watch and saw that it read 9:33PM. My stomach dropped. I had slept straight through the daylight entirely and don't remember one bit of it. How was that possible? No wonder Raven was giving me the death glare; she hadn't been fed or let out all day. I attended to that immediately.

I felt fine while I was watching Raven running around in the backyard, but eventually the voices started coming back to me and filling me with an anxiety bordering on nausea. I let Raven inside and started pacing the living room, trying to regain control over my own mind. The terrible sound of the cacophony of alien utterings, the unspeakable desolation of the images they filled my mind with – I could feel it slowly but surely destroying the flimsy grip I had left of my sanity. And yet, I knew I had to go back there. The light was calling to me. I had to see it for what it truly was. I had to understand what this force was that was interacting with me. I don't believe I any longer had a choice.

I found myself, for the third night in a row, taking a turn at the end of my driveway and looking up towards the mansion at the end of the street. Like clockwork, that top floor window was illuminated yet again with its unusual golden glow. I was ready to figure out what was going on inside that room. I began my trek in its direction.

As I got closer to the source, I could feel the voices getting louder and louder within me. I couldn't even hear my own footsteps any longer over its hideous sound. As I reached the edge of the front lawn of the mansion, the discordant chorus of this unearthly chattering became absolutely deafening, and I couldn't help any longer but scream out in agony. The visions in my head of that dark world of unimaginable horrors became so clear that it was becoming increasingly difficult to distinguish that vile realm from reality. But still, the unworldly light coming from that window shone through brighter than all the layers of hazy imagery that floated in my consciousness, and acted as the beacon that guided me onward.

My head swimming in a pandemonic chaos, I proceeded past the old, flaking picket fence that protected the place from outsiders for over 50 years, and began to walk towards the front entrance of the mansion. I reached the door, or the decayed, crumbling fragment of what was once a door, and, without a second thought, broke through the frail barrier of wood and dust and stepped into the interior of the dark mansion.

The blackness inside was almost overwhelming. I could only see that which was illuminated by the reflecting light of the moon that shone through the opened doorway. It irradiated enough to show me the beginnings of a winding, disintegrating staircase marked by dusty marble columns of Gothic styling. I took a few slow steps up the stairs and my very limited light source from the doorway was no longer of any help. The all-encompassing darkness was now uninterruptedly filled by the broken, discontinuous images that floated in my mind of the horrible, indescribable beings who hovered along the alien wasteland of unending bleakness, accompanied by those sickening voices of unknowable tongue. I walked up the creaky stairs without knowing who or what was guiding my steps and where exactly they were taking me. As I proceeded further and further up, I could begin to hear a strange, droning ambience that grew in power the further I ascended. This told me I was getting closer.

When I finally reached the end of the staircase and onto the top floor, I could see from which room the mysterious light was coming from. There was a closed room at the end of the hall where I could see the golden light seeping through the bottom of the door. This was also where that odd hum was coming from, overpowering the atmosphere and vibrating the hallway with its reverberation. I felt an unnerving chill creep over my body and a sudden fright fill my heart, but I found myself getting closer and closer to the door. Mere steps away from it, the voices, the visions, and the droning were all reaching a crescendo that was bringing my head to the brink of explosion. The force of it all was unbearable. I yelled out in torment as I put my hand on the doorknob and forcefully pushed the door open. What I saw inside was beyond comprehension.

I was blinded by the magnificent golden light that was now unrestricted and utterly permeated everything in sight, but through heavily squinted eyes I tried to make out what was before me. The light was streaming out of a giant, opened book that sat on a table in the middle of the room, occupied by a large, wretched, hideous remnant of a man, whose partially incorporeal form was almost entirely consumed by this light to the point where it was infused into his very being. He was hunched over, writing madly into this book, scribbling away hysterically as if possessed by an unfathomable force. There were a dozen or so decomposed bodies that laid about the edges of the bloodstained room, some of which resembling beings that didn't look entirely human. The chaotic symphony of disembodied voices was as loud and clear as ever, and seemed to have absolute control over the incomprehensibly repulsive being who wrote in it. That pulsing drone that wobbled the entire room was a result of the sheer power of the force that cascaded from the book. All of it came from that book.

That spectral monster of light and wretchedness turned around, and he looked directly into my eyes with a look of such unutterable evil and cruelness that my heart froze in terror. I tried to let out a scream but no sound would come. He stood up, and slowly reached out his arm toward me. The light amplified beyond conception, and then everything went white ...

Astral Entanglement

Edward floated around weightlessly, observing the boundless space around him with wonder. No matter which direction he looked, everything was permeated in a deep, dark blue. There were no walls, ceilings, or floors. And yet, still, there was coherent settlement, there was intelligent organization; there was civilization. Perhaps countless civilizations, laid out all around him, stretching out as far as infinity stretched. There was no measurable end to this dimension, and one would need endless incarnations to explore its vastness and reach any definitive grasp of what was there.

Each time Edward entered, he could only explore an infinitesimal fraction of it, before he would remember his body lying down on a padded mattress in his instructor McHale's practice room back in Providence, Rhode Island, and then he would come rushing back to it involuntarily and his adventure would be over. McHale always stressed that the two things that bring an astral projector back against his will were remembering his physical body, and fear. Predictably, both of these things were difficult to avoid when one was out in the field. While mankind had come by now to have learned quite a bit about the astral realms in 2053, they were still dealing largely with the vast unknown, and fear of the unknown was the most inescapable fear of all, especially when your very soul was at stake.

Edward pushed himself along in the direction of the pulsating neon pyramids that hovered in the distance, situated between magnificent castles and glowing obelisks and towers all around, with lighted pathways connecting them all. The structures on the astral realm appeared upon sight to possess the same type of solidity that ones in the physical world did; it was only when you got close enough to make contact with them that you learned you could float right through them. Edward remembered McHale had said that everything on the astral dimension was created and manifested from the minds of other projectors since the beginning of human history, at least. This place was like one giant collective imagination of the human race.

He watched other projectors gliding in and out of the pyramids below him, and just when he made his move to join them, he felt a sharp tugging on his back, as if his spine had a rope tied to it and was being fiercely pulled. He knew what this meant.

Edward suddenly found himself back in his body, back on Earth, with McHale sitting calmly in his seat at the front of the sleek, white room, typing into his logs. Edward looked around to see if Howard was still there — his friend that he had brought to this place for the first time today, in the hopes of giving him his first astral experience. He saw Howard lying in the bed to the right of him, watching him intently, clearly in-body. Edward darted his eyes back to the front of the room.

"McHale, did you pull me out?" asked Edward.

"Yes, I did," said McHale.

"Why'd you do that? I barely got to see anything!" said Edward, sitting himself up on his bed.

"I could sense your friend Howard here was growing way too anxious. I felt it was time for us to give him what he came for," replied McHale, with his signature smirk creeping onto his face.

"Oh, fine. You gonna give him that classic speech first?"

"To the both of you, yes."

"Huh? Howard and I are going together?" asked Edward.

"Joint-projection, yes. For his first time, at least, I figured he could use a knowledgeable and experienced guide such as yourself," said McHale.

"Oh, how very flattering of you, McHale," said

Edward. "Alrighty then. Let's eat this frog."

"Are you ready, Howard?" asked McHale.

"I think so. I'm as ready as I ever will be, sir," replied Howard.

"You're a good kid, Howard, but you can cut it out with that 'sir' shit right about now," said McHale with a warm smile. "Alright, scoot your beds closer together, lie down, and I'll connect your hands."

Edward and Howard did as he said. McHale then walked in between their beds, grabbed Edward's right hand and Howard's left hand, pressed them together, and then wrapped them up securely with white straps specifically designed for joint-projection work. This way, their energy fields were connected to each other's, and sufficiently intertwined to act as one astral vehicle. After he was done, McHale returned to his position at the front of the room.

"Alright, fellas. First and foremost, quiet your minds. Use the counting and deep breathing technique, and let your minds enter the meditative state."

McHale stood quietly for a few moments before continuing.

"You are about to embark on a journey into the astral realms. The astral realms are an other-dimensional, energetically generated, incorporeal, multi-layered, ethereal plane of existence connected metaphysically to the universal consciousness of planet Earth. Existing on a dimension of reality separate from our own, these astral realms deviate entirely from our own dimension's laws of physics. A successful astral projector is one who is effectively able to make the mental and physical transition from *our* laws of physics to *their* laws of physics."

McHale paused for a moment before continuing, observing Edward and Howard's breathing pace.

"All the different dimensions of reality are merely frequencies, in the same way that different radio stations are frequencies. In the same way that your radio is in one physical location, yet can access any frequency by simply turning a dial, the human body also remains in its one physical location, and yet can access a vast array of frequencies within existence, if only we shift our own dials. That is precisely what we've learned to do."

Edward felt himself drifting more and more into the desired meditative state, his breathing and heartrate slowing. McHale's voice had a hypnotizing effect on him.

"When I turn on the frequency generator, it will emit a droning pulse of sound that mathematically matches the exact frequency of the astral realm, which will allow your brains to synchronize with it and make the proper connection, overriding the frequency of our Earthly realm. Your entire perception will shift from the one realm to the other, allowing your consciousness-generated astral body free agency on the new realm to experience it with no restraints. Because your physical body is where your consciousness currently makes its residence, your consciousness can only remain out of body in another realm for so long, before its forced back to its current home. This is your body's long-developed survival mechanism. This is why astral projections are limited to only a couple Earth hours at a time, yet it will feel like much longer on the astral realm, so no rushing is necessary in your exploration of its mysteries."

"It is now time to see for yourself. Prepare to transcend space and time."

And with that, McHale concluded his send off, put on a special set of thickly padded headphones, and flipped a switch on his device.

Edward felt butterflies rise within his stomach as the frequency generator let out its high-pitched hum. As it droned on, he felt his body begin to slowly become enveloped in what seemed like buzzing electrical vibrations all over. He knew that this was his energy field transitioning from one dimension to another.

Once every inch of his body was taken over by the buzzing feeling, he knew that the connection between his energy field and Howard's was completely synchronized, acting as one, and ready to be collectively separated from their physical bodies. Edward was taught to produce this separation by starting from the top to the bottom, so he started with urging his head forward; not his physical head, but the part of his energy field that resided within the space of his head, until he felt a definite separation. Once clear, Edward then continued the process at the shoulders, then the chest, then the waist, pelvis, and downwards, an increasing feeling of exhilarating liberation at each point. He found that the feet were the toughest of all to energetically separate; it was the energy field's last desperate attempt to stay contained within the physical vessel, but once Edward fully detached them from each other, his astral body was then free to roam unrestricted within the astral dimension. With one last fleeting effort, they finally broke free.

Edward found himself at his usual starting point, just a short distance away from the mysterious, pulsating neon pyramids that always intrigued him. He looked to his right and saw Howard floating beside him, looking absolutely mesmerized at the spectacle that lay before him. Howard turned to Edward and, without vocalizing, telepathically said to him "This … is … insane. This is more amazing than I ever imagined! Are those the pyramids you mentioned before?"

"Of course. Want to go inside them? I've never even done it before myself."

"You bet your ass I do!"

Edward laughed, not remembering Howard to ever let out a cuss word before. Apparently astral projection could bring someone out of their shell in more ways than one, he thought.

Howard rushed off in the direction of the pyramids, turning backwards to face Edward as he zoomed closer towards them, gesturing for him to catch up. Edward sped on after him.

They reached the entrance together, and Howard floated right on in without hesitation. Edward quickly followed him in. He found himself in a long, grand hallway, permeated in a misty, green glow all over, guarded by dark, cloaked beings positioned all along each side. Howard was nowhere in sight.

Edward proceeded on down the hallway, a hint of uneasiness creeping up within him. How could Howard disappear that quickly? He saw a large black door at the end of the hallway, guarded by yet more cloaked beings, and wondered if Howard was inside there. He floated along toward the door and made it to within a few feet from it before three of the cloaked guards rushed up in front of him, blocking his way. He tried to look under their hoods and get a glimpse of their faces but he could only see blackness there. He struggled to push past them, but then suddenly found himself completely paralyzed, as if he was frozen in space. He didn't understand how, but he knew that these cloaked beings somehow did this to him. Edward couldn't move his astral body one bit, but mentally he was becoming overwhelmed with enraged panic.

"What have you done to me?! Who are you people?! What did you do to my friend?!"

They remained facing his direction, staring into his soul through black, formless faces, completely still, and offered no response of any kind.

Just then, from somewhere within the room that the black door guarded, Edward heard a horrible, bloodcurdling scream that sounded as if someone was being tortured beyond their wildest nightmares. He knew it was Howard. Terror shot up within him.

He immediately felt himself slammed back into his physical body, suddenly back in McHale's room. He abruptly jumped up from his bed. He looked over at Howard's physical body and found it disturbingly still. He didn't see him breathing. He frantically looked up to the front of the room and saw that McHale was nowhere to be found.

He turned back to Howard, reached over and lightly slapped him in the face a few times. No response.

He put his fingers on Howard's neck and checked his pulse.

No response.

The Painting

David walked through the garden, as the light Spring rain sprinkled down upon the lilacs and daffodils and crocuses. This rain, coupled with the gentle wind that stirred amidst the trees, only accentuated the rich scents of the flowers. He was taking the scenic route through his friend Edmund's estate, who had begged for David to come see him immediately. Edmund was very wealthy (due to his inheritance from his aristocratic father), and liked to collect great works of art, and he couldn't wait to show David the latest addition to his collection. He liked to keep it a bit of a surprise, so that David's always-indulgent reaction would be all the more pleasurable.

David walked in through the open door at the edge of the garden, as a housemaid came to greet him and take his coat and hat. He wore a white tucked-in dress shirt with brown trousers. She led him up the stairs to Edmund's art room, and motioned for him to take a seat in front of what appeared to be a massive, covered canvas that took up the entire side of the room. She left to call on Edmund.

I guess this is it, David thought. He sat looking at the thing, knowing he could easily just lift up the cover and see what all the fuss was about, but what was the honor in that? He would never want to be unappreciative of Edmund's hospitality, even if just in principal. David's astonishment was a currency that Edmund's joy seemed to thrive on, and it wouldn't do well to spoil its genuineness. So he sat and waited patiently, anxiety boiling up inside him as his imagination coursed through the possibilities of what lie beneath.

"Curious, aren't you?" said Edmund, as he silently glided in through the doorway with a smile. He looked as splendid as ever, with his neatly poofed-up hair, vibrant blue eyes, and elaborately decorated waistcoat.

"Why yes, quite by design, wouldn't you say?" said David with a chuckle. He hoped that didn't come off as sounding unindulgent.

"By design, indeed! However, do you mean to say you would *not* be curious, if not for my theatrics?" said Edmund, narrowing his eyes in an exaggerated fashion.

"I knew you'd say that. No, no, my dear Edmund, that's not what I mean!" said David.

"Well, know I said *this*! The painting that stands enshrouded before us has just been removed from the Louvre Museum in Paris to take residence here in my home! The *Louvre*, David!"

"My goodness. Is that even possible? How did you manage that?" said David.

"With enough money and rhetorical prowess, my friend, all things are possible. This painting costed more than I could comfortably dream, and for it, I dreamed more than I could comfortably afford." said Edmund.

"I'm positive that makes no sense. But no matter! How about we unveil it then, no?" said David.

"Only with the proper introduction!" said Edmund, positioning himself. "Behold! *The Death of Sardanapalus* by Eugène Delacroix, 1827!"

With that, Edmund dramatically pulled the cover off the wall-sized painting, revealing the art in all its splendor. Lush with deep reds and browns, it showed an Assyrian king lounging back on a bed, while all around him in his room naked captive women were being raped and stabbed and used as decorative ornaments by his soldiers. Its savagery was matched only by its beauty.

"What do you think?" said Edmund, his breath held in suspense.

David stood silent and expressionless for a long moment, his eyes darting around the massive surface of the painting, taking everything in. Edmund was nearly quivering in anticipation.

David's blank face finally erupted in an expression that could only be interpreted as utter disgust.

"I'm ... flabbergasted, frankly. Edmund, what in the world would possess you to want to own such an image of depravity?"

Edmund took a step back, looking almost wounded.

"My dear David! I'm not sure I know what you mean!" said Edmund. "What about this incredible work of art revolts you so?"

"What about it *doesn't*?! Just look at the wretched thing! A celebration of pure violence and brutality, and indifference about it all! Are these the kinds of things your soul resonates with?" asked David.

"In a way, absolutely!" said Edmund.

"Edmund! How could you say that?" said David, incredulous. "'In a way?' What do you mean?!"

"David, my soul is made up of violence and brutality and indifference just as much as it is made up of peacefulness and gentleness and compassion. And so is yours!" said Edmund.

"Like hell it is!" said David. "What evidence do you hold that gives you reason to believe my soul is associated with such immorality?"

"Exactly, like hell it is! And like heaven it is too! David, my beloved friend, please forgive me, but you don't really believe in such a concept as hazy and baseless as 'immorality,' do you?"

"Hazy? Baseless? Morality is anything but! Are you telling me you don't believe in morality? In good deeds and bad deeds? These things are concrete!" said David.

"To you, these things are concrete, but to me, these things are water! Or perhaps fog! One man's good deed is another man's atrocity, and one man's bad deed is another man's miracle! Who are we to swing down such a gavel of judgment upon human acts, as if we're operating from some omniscient position and can decide for all of mankind?" said Edmund. He turned his eyes back to the painting, as if looking for confirmation.

"We don't need to operate from an omniscient position, because God already does for us! He has already laid these things out for us! Does the word of God mean nothing to you?" said David, looking like he was nearing tears.

"Not nothing, but certainly not everything! In fact, it only means as much to me as the word of Osiris, and the word of Zeus, and the word of Buddha, and the word of Shiva, and the word of Odin, and the word of Anu, and ... need I go on? There's so bloody many of them that it cheapens the value of all of them! And guess what? They all hold a different set of values, a different standard of morality!" said Edmund with a triumphant smirk on his face.

David just stood and stared in disbelief, his mouth half-open. For a moment, the birds chirping outside was the only sound that could be heard in the room.

"I … I don't think I've ever heard such monstrous garbage in my entire life. I can't believe you, Edmund. I just can't believe you would align yourself with such a deplorable philosophy. The philosophy of a degenerate!"

"The philosophy of *reality*, David," said Edmund. "The simple truth of the matter that so few are brave enough to acknowledge. You people cling on to your gods and your dogmas and your "rules" and your stigmas, forgetting the very multiplicity of it all, the relativity of it all, the fabrication of it all. Every single bit of it was just made up by groups of random men throughout time that you'll never know the faces of!"

David laughed sardonically, shaking his head. He had nothing for him.

"Can you at least admit that these rich reds and browns are some of the most splendidly rendered tones you've ever seen in a painting?" asked Edmund with a charming smile.

And with that, David walked out of the room.

He marched down the stairs, grabbed his coat and his hat, and walked back out into the garden.

The rain from earlier had dissipated, leaving behind a pleasant smell and a lush moisture to the air and the grass. The sun was out and shining now, poking its head through a break in the trees and illuminating the grounds with an almost unnaturally golden tone. This light poured onto the flowers and their vibrant colors reflected into a dreamy mist that surrounded them like an aura. David stood still, bathing in a shower of purple and golden glow.

For the first time in his life, he contemplated committing suicide.

The Desert of Xibalba

A wind blew over me, and I was able to feel the dust within it, scraping over my skin. Slowly, so very slowly, I opened my eyes, which was something I hadn't expected to do again. Chosen as the sacrifice, I knew what was to come. Everyone knew. Once every five years someone would be chosen, and I was the one. My life had been long enough, so it was right that I was taken rather than a child. As I began to move, I found my usual bodily discomforts were gone. It was strange. Uncertainty sweeping through me, I looked around. All around me there was mist, so I couldn't see far away, and yet when I looked up there were stars. So very luminous. None of them were anything like the stars of the place I had called home.

Carefully, wondering if the wind would be strong enough to push me, I moved, standing where I'd been sitting, looking around once more. There was nothing other than the mist around me, although, as I looked more closely at it, I found myself wondering if it truly was mist. Maybe it was something else. I had no knowledge of what the world of the dead was supposed to be like, but that could well have been where I'd ended up. Especially as I wasn't sure where it was I should go next. Only the longer I stood there the easier it became to see through the mist, to see what was around me. From what I could see, I was standing on a platform of rock, everything around me dark, and I didn't know if there was anywhere to go from there. At least until I realized the darkness was fading too. It was interesting that I could see more the longer I was there. Something to understand, in the future, if I did indeed have a future ahead of me. I hoped I did.

When the darkness fully dissipated, I could see platforms all around me. Some of them had shapes on them, that could have been bodies, but I had no way of knowing. Not from where I was standing. These rock platforms were raised high in the sky, so there had to be some kind of way down that didn't involve jumping. Not knowing what might happen if I got too close to the edge of the platform, I moved slowly forward, breathing in deeply as I did, trying not to let my fear of the unknown get the better of me. I almost had before. Lying on the slab, looking up at our shaman, I'd felt my heart beating hard in my chest, from the lack of knowledge I had of what was to come. What I'd been told didn't matter. It wasn't until I experienced death for myself that I'd understand.

Upon reaching the edge, I was able to see a set of steps carved into the rock. Getting to them wasn't going to be simple, but it was possible. I had two options. I could stay where I was, with no food, water, or shelter, or I could try the steps, and see where they might take me. Part of me didn't want to go anywhere. I was meant to be dead. I wasn't meant to be standing in the sky on a rock platform surrounded by other rock platforms ... unless, of course, what I was experiencing was death. How was I supposed to know? I wasn't a shaman, so I'd never been taught about the afterlife, or the other worlds, and that meant everything I was experiencing was new. There were those who said that death would test those who arrived there, to see if they were worthy of the end, and those who weren't would have to live through another life. Was that what would happen to me? I had many questions, that I might never get the answer to, if I let myself stay on the platform. I needed to make the decision to move.

So that was what I did. Ignoring the fear that would have stopped me in life, I sat on the edge of the platform, and reached out carefully with one foot. When that foot touched the step, I let myself drop, hoping that would be enough to keep me from dropping down to wherever the ground was. Breathing in deeply, grateful when I did find myself on the step, I slowly made my way down them, thinking about where I was. The wind was still blowing hard, dust still scraping at my skin, but it didn't hurt as much as I thought it should. Maybe it was another part of the test, if there even was a test. The further down I went, the less sure I was of what I was doing. I didn't have any other options. All I could do was keep moving, in the hope things would work themselves out once I did reach the ground.

Instead, I found myself in a maze of rock. The steps I'd made my way down disappeared entirely when I looked back at them, which was not something I'd expected to happen. Biting down hard on my lip, I worked to convince myself everything would work out. Somehow. I was being tested, nothing more, and every step I took was going to be a step toward me finding out where exactly I was, and what my next steps needed to be. Giving myself a mental push, I started moving through the maze. The wind was less biting, probably due to the rock all around me. I could still feel the dust within it, and from what was under my bare feet, the only logical explanation for it was sand. It got between my toes, but it never stuck there, like it would have done had my feet been sweating. Everything about the experience was unusual, but then that was what I should have expected. The unusual. With every step I took, all I could do was hope I was closer to the end of the maze.

Eventually, after what truly seemed to be hours to me, I did step out of the maze, and found myself surrounded by a desert. All I could see for miles was sand. No sign of anything else. No sign of there being life anywhere near me. Turning, wondering if I'd come the wrong way through the maze, I found the maze itself had disappeared. Sand was everywhere. I could see it for miles in front of me, miles behind me, miles to both sides of me, and it was harder than I wanted it to be to make the decision to keep going. I knew it was what I had to do. Breathing in deeply, doing my best to stay calm, I slowly looked around me. There was nothing to tell me where I should be going. Nothing in the sand. Yet I knew I had to make the decision to move, because otherwise I was just going to be stuck there.

North, to me, was the direction I chose. I walked through the sand, my feet and legs never seeming to tire. I never seemed to get hungry or thirsty, so maybe I really was dead, but if I was I had no idea how I'd found myself in a desert. Nothing in my life had been anything like the desert around me. Unless, of course, I was actually trapped in some kind of a dream, one my mind had created for me, in order for me to have some kind of death. Yet that didn't make any real sense. My mind would have died with the rest of me.

We knew that from the way the world had been before the destruction. Even though we'd gone back to the old ways, we still remembered what we had learned before, and we combined the two; superstition mixing with knowledge, which, to us, wasn't a bad thing. Maybe those who'd once called our world home would see things differently, but they were gone, their way of living having changed everything for everyone. That was how I'd ended up in a desert. It had to be.

The further I went the more confused I became. How was I still moving? How was my body still going, without me feeling at all tired? I kept going, because it was all I could do, in the hope I would find something. Or someone. Anything was preferable to all the sand around me. Every step I took I tried to convince myself I was one step closer to something, and yet the only thing around me was sand. Just what I wanted. Taking a deep breath, telling myself things would work themselves out in the end, I kept moving forward. Kept putting one foot in front of the other. If it was a test, then I was going to prove myself, and if it wasn't … well, there had to be something somewhere.

***

Before I reached the city, it was possible I had been walking for days. That was truly what it felt like. Yet when I reached the city, when I stepped onto the first piece of stone I'd felt since the platform, I turned to look at how far I'd come. In the distance, far closer than it had seemed to me, was the maze I'd come through made visible again. I was even more certain than I was before that I'd been tested. Walking for so long was nothing more than the afterlife seeing what I'd be willing to do. Had things been different I wouldn't have been willing to walk anywhere near as far as I had, but I wasn't going to stop in the middle of a desert. The city, I hoped, would be somewhere I could rest for a while, before I made the decision as to what I'd do next. Was there anything more I could do?

Wind, like it had done before, whistled through the streets, and that was the only thing I found in the entire place. There were no people, just buildings, and they were nothing like the buildings I'd left behind back home. Some of them looked almost as though they'd been crafted from stone, rather than made out of bricks, but I couldn't tell how that would have been done. The city wasn't carved into a mountain … unless there had once been a mountain, and something had happened to it. I had no way of knowing, until I found the building I hoped I'd find: the library. The bookcases, like everything else, were made of stone. That wasn't the strangest part. All the books I'd been expecting were actually stone tablets. Carefully, not certain how old they were, I removed one of them from the bookcase, to find it was blank. Had it been blank when it was put on the shelf? Feeling the first faint tendrils of panic I made my way around the bookcases, checking every one of those stone tablets. Every single one of them was blank.

One tablet sat on the librarian's desk, and I made my way over to it, not believing for a moment I'd see anything on it. Then I realized there was something. Symbols that meant nothing to me. Tears welling up in my eyes, even though I tried to hold back all the emotions, I reached out to take the tablet, to have a closer look. As I did the symbols changed. I'd never seen anything like it before. It was a reminder that I wasn't at home any longer. I was on another world, and there was no way I could know what would happen to me next. The way things had happened had proved to me that this place was very different from where I'd come from. Finally, the symbols became words I could understand.

"You have found yourself here for a reason. The next step to take is to find out what that reason is."

Helpful. I stared at it, waiting for something more, only for it to stay exactly like that. Dropping it back onto the desk it cracked in half. Part of me didn't care. Yet I knew, with certainty, I wasn't anywhere I'd been before, and destroying things that belonged to others wasn't something I was willing to do. Carefully, I picked up the two parts of the tablet. Holding them, I could feel something more than I had before, maybe because they were broken, but again that was another question I didn't have an answer to. Holding the two bits of tablet close, I urged it to fix itself. That wasn't something I would ever have been able to do back at home, and it wasn't something I truly believed would work here, until, unexpectedly, it did. The tablet was whole once more. Looking down at it, I could see the same words I had seen before, but they didn't irritate me the way they did before. Something had happened to me.

Much more gently than before, I put the tablet down. I knew that what I needed to do more than anything was rest, so I made my way out of the library. I looked around the desolate street, eventually spotting a house that seemed like it would have a bed in it. I wasn't sure I wanted to sleep in someone else's bed, but I felt tired then, like putting the tablet back together had taken a lot out of me. The bed wasn't anything like one of the beds I'd left behind either. When I lay down I assumed I'd be able to feel the rock it was made of, but I didn't. Instead it seemed soft, like there was something other than rock making up part of it, and maybe that was the case. Running my tongue over my dry lips, I told myself I'd be able to find some answers to the questions I had when I woke up.

***

Sound was what woke me. The kind of sound I would have woken up to at home, before I died, and, slowly, I pushed myself out of the bed. No one else was in the house I'd chosen, so I stepped out the door. For the first time since I'd arrived, I found myself looking at other people. At least they seemed to be people to begin with, until I started to look more closely, and then I knew there was something more to what they were.

They looked like people because that was what made the most sense to my brain. I could understand it, and yet I still pushed to see them as they truly were, rather than as I needed them to be. As I did this, I found myself looking at creatures that I would have normally called animals. Only they were acting the way my people would have done, during the first part of the day, and I could see the sun slowly rising over the buildings. It was much redder than our sun. Everything about what I was experiencing was strange, but that didn't mean it wasn't something that was supposed to happen.

No one looked at me when I stepped out of the house. "Hello?" I could hear the fear in my own voice, and I did my best to push it away. "Can someone help me?"

There was no response. It was almost as though I wasn't really there, and there was a chance that was the case. Before I'd slept, the entire place had been empty. Waking up to find things so different was jarring. Slowly, doing my best not to walk into anyone, even though they seemed to be able to walk straight through me, I made my way to the library. That was the only place I could think I might be able to get some answers. If there were people around now, I stood a better chance of making sense of all those stone tablets. When I stepped into the building, however, everything was different. The stone tablets were gone, replaced by the kinds of books I'd believed would be there the first time, and the bookcases were now made of wood. Bizarre. I slowly looked around. I was the only one there, it seemed. That wasn't a bad thing, necessarily, but I knew my lack of understanding was making things harder for me.

"I was told to expect you." The voice, male, made me jump. "I am Balam, and I'm here to welcome you."

Doing my best to stay calm, I turned to look at him. Balam looked like a jaguar, mostly, apart from when he looked just like the shaman of my village. "Welcome me?"

"You have been chosen," he said as he studied me. "It is not unheard of, but in order for you to find your place here, you need to give an offering to our gods."

"How can I give an offering when I have nothing?"

"Everyone has something, whether or not they realize that." His eyes met with mine. "I will take you to them, so you can work out what it is you have, and then you may call this world home."

"What if I don't want to do that?" I said. "I'm supposed to be dead right now."

Balam raised an eyebrow. "You are dead. That's why I'm here." He stared at me. "I understand this isn't how you assumed death would be, but that was your mistake. Death is complicated, my friend, and you will learn what it means as you find yourself a place here." He stepped closer. "The sooner we go the better it will be for everyone."

Before I could respond he was leaving the library, and I knew the only thing I could do was follow him. As we made our way through the crowded streets people nodded to him, because they were able to see him, while I was still a ghost. Maybe it was better that way. I had no reason to call this new place home. There were things I wanted to say to him, but I couldn't find the words I needed. Things I wanted to ask him. Everything about being there was so different to how I'd expected it to be. Sighing, I brushed a hand through my hair, and that was when he glanced back at me, his eyes meeting with mine for a moment. Nodding, he turned back to look at where we were going.

"Going through this kind of change is never going to be simple," he said. "You were a death that wasn't truly meant to happen, no matter what it is you might think, so you have another chance here. It's going to be a different life to the one you were living before. This world … it's for those who have no other place to go yet. It was created by those who understood death in a way that most don't."

"Purgatory?"

"Maybe, for your people, this would be how it seemed, but it's not truly that. It's not a place where you're going to be trapped forever. Just until the end of your natural life here." He glanced back a second time. "I would say you have a good thirty to forty years left, at least. You may have believed your life was over, but it wasn't."

***

We stopped in front of a giant stone head that floated above the sand. Balam put a hand on my shoulder. "This is where I leave you, my friend."

He was gone when I'd realized there were still things I wanted to ask him, my focus much more on the head than it was on anything else. It reminded me of the god I'd been sacrificed to. Had I found myself on his world? For a long time, nothing happened. I just stood in front of a floating head that did nothing, and then I felt it. I couldn't put my finger on exactly what it was, but the head was different, and it looked at me in the same way I'd looked at it. I could feel it analyzing me. Unwillingly, I took a step back, the fear I felt getting the better of me, because being around something like that wasn't something I could ever have imagined.

"Of course you couldn't have imagined this." The voice sounded amused, the mouth of the face moving in a way I wouldn't have thought was possible if I hadn't seen it. "Nothing about this is what you expected, is it? Death was meant to be a specific way, but you were chosen to be sacrificed, due to your age, and that was what brought you here. Like your people, you believed you would be of no use to them. Only you would have been. That's why I made the decision to bring you here. They took away time you needed to have, and that's not something I can forgive."

"It was better to choose me. I had made it to adulthood, and the children, who might have been chosen, had so much still in front of them."

"You aren't wrong. But I never once asked for these sacrifices, and that is something I am still displeased about. Many things have been misread, misinterpreted, which is what has led to this happening. In time, it will become much more complicated. That is why this place exists."

"Bringing me here was the better option?"

"This world was created for those who are different, and you know as well as I do that you were always different. You were nothing like the people you called friends. That was part of the reason you were chosen. Your shaman made his choice based on who he thought should not have been born in the first place. Your age ... well, it just made it easier for him to make that choice without someone arguing against it, especially as you were happy enough to go through with it. I understand why. Yet I still need to do what I can to stop this from happening. You are here to learn more than the others, before going back to teach them the lessons you will be taught by me."

"I …"

"Now is not the time to argue. You were told you would need to present me a gift, and that is what I ask of you. That is what is required for you to learn here, before returning to the other world, to be my shaman. To change what is happening."

"Why me?"

"You are the best person for this." The head appeared to smile. "Of course you can't understand that yet, but you will, and I am glad I was able to bring you here. There are those who've given up without even trying to get off the stone platforms, but I understand, this is not a normal world. I'm not surprised that's the choice they made." I felt his power touch me then. "You are going to walk this path, because once it is done you will have peace, and I will make certain of that."

"Don't I get a chance to think about this?"

"By doing this, you will save the lives of the children you care about. Walking this path, for your people, is not going to be easy, but it is necessary. I can show you what's to come, if you wish me to. I know how this ends, because it has happened before, and that is the reason this world exists. That's the reason the town is full of the people you saw. I brought them here so they would have a chance to live. They are the people you will save, if you do as I ask of you now."

***

Balam was waiting for me when I returned to town. His eyes met with mine, and we looked at each other for a long time. I don't know what I was waiting for, what I was expecting, but I was waiting for something. Finally, breathing in deeply, he gestured for me to follow him, so I did. Upon reaching the library, he looked at me once more. "You know who I was." He looked down. "I know you can see past the image I now wear to the person I was before, and that is a sign you are the one we were waiting for. The one who can save us from this fate." He looked back up at me. "We've been waiting for a long time. Longer than you can know. I was beginning to think this day would never come."

For a moment, I didn't know how to respond. "I died before you."

"Did you?" He smiled. "I'm not certain that is the case, but maybe I'm wrong. I believe my soul died long before you did, and yet I know what you mean, because my body was still there when you were chosen to be sacrificed. I remember looking down at you, knife in hand, so certain I was making the best choiceI could for our people, as that was what I'd been told by those who came before. By the shamans who passed the mantle down to me. I was teaching my successor the same thing. My beliefs were so deeply entrenched I couldn't see the mistakes I was making."

"What happens if I make the decision not to help?"

"Like the rest of us you'll have to wait forthe next person to be asked. I was asked. Saying yes was the only logical thing for me to do, and yet I didn't say yes. Instead, I said I couldn't. I wasn't willing to walk that path, because even then I couldn't see what I'd done. It wasn't until the souls started gathering here that I realized the mistake I'd made. I have been angry with myself for that for a very long time." He sighed. "I was called long before you were, but you are the one I believe should be walking that path. The one who could find the truth."

Slowly, I nodded, although that didn't mean I was going to be willing to do what he wanted me to do. "I understand what you're saying. What I don't understand is why it should be me. Why I'm here after you. Nothing about this makes any sense."

"Death is always confusing. It's even more confusing when the gods step in to make certain changes. This is where we were gathered, to save our souls, and this is where we will stay, until someone is willing to do that. We need you, in a way we've never needed anyone before. I wouldn't be asking this of you if I didn't believe it was the only option we had." He looked into my eyes. "I will help you, because I made that promise to myself. I will never give up on the chance of being able to fix the damage I caused. Please give me this chance." He reached out to put a hand on my shoulder. "I am sorry for what I did, for the choices I made, and for taking your life long before I should have."

Again, I found myself not knowing how to respond. I thought of arguments I'd heard that I shouldn't have, as I lay waiting for my death to come. How the shaman, Balam, had argued for there being more sacrifices. How he believed we weren't doing enough for our god.

"What happened after I died?"

"Things changed, the way I was trying to make happen. We called for at least one sacrifice a year. Most of those were young people, and they've almost all ended up here. When I first arrived, they hated me for what I'd done, and I understand that. I am grateful they gave me a chance in the end, even though I'm not certain I truly deserved it." He shrugged. "What I need now is for you to help me, and to help our god, so this doesn't happen anymore. It seems to me like more of the spirits of the dead gather here with each passing day. I believe what I did changed everything in ways it should never have been changed, and all I can do now is beg for forgiveness. Please help our people. Please do what I couldn't."

"How many have arrived since I did?"

"I have met three, but I know of five. I believe, from what they said, our beliefs have passed from one people to another, and the more that happens, the more of the dead will gather here. Make your choice, so the next can come if you aren't willing to do something more than I did."

Once more I nodded, feeling the weight of those people on my shoulders. If I'd fought against my sacrifice would that have changed things?

"I will do what I can to help, but I'm not making any promises that doing it will actually change anything. I am only one person, Balam, and there's no way we can be certain I will be enough."

"You will. I was only one person, and I was enough to force this change on people. The time will come when you will be enough to make them change once more." With his words, the library around us had transformed again. "Our god has heard you, and now the time has come for us to prepare for what you will be doing next. For how you will fix the damage I caused."

Looking around slowly, I asked myself if I'd made the right choice. "I will do the best I can. That's all anyone can ever do."

Tron lives.

Coming Soon by Brandon Tezzano

Posthuman Odyssey

You Were Wrong About Me

Indigo Musings

My Secret Muse

The Morphean Labyrinth

About the Author

Brandon Tezzano lives in Baltimore, Maryland. When he is not writing perplexing literature, he creates music, films, and digital paintings. He holds degrees in English and Film, and is currently pursuing a Doctorate.

CPSIA information can be obtained
at www.ICGtesting.com
Printed in the USA
LVHW090833041119
636238LV00008B/943/P

9 780578 570105